A row of fluffy ducklings...

waddle behind their mother duck.
She's heading toward more...

DUCKS!

BY GAIL GIBBONS

HOLIDAY HOUSE • NEW YORK

FOR CLAIRE COUNIHAN

SPECIAL THANKS TO
BRYAN SWIFT,
Waterfowl Specialist
of the Wildlife Resources Center,
Wildlife Services,
Delmar, New York

Library of Congress Cataloging-in-Publicaion Data
Gibbons, Gail.
Ducks! / by Gail Gibbons.—1st ed.
p.   cm.
ISBN 0-8234-1567-8
1. Ducks—Juvenile literature. [1. Ducks.] I. Title.
QL696.A52 G53 2001
598.4'1—dc21
00–032003

A female duck
is called a HEN.

A male duck
is called a
DRAKE.

FEATHERS

WEBBED
FEET

MALLARD

Ducks are one member of the water bird family called waterfowl.
Waterfowl have two important characteristics in common. They have
webbed feet to help them swim and dive, and their feathers are
waterproof.

When a duck oils its feathers it is PREENING.

PREEN GLAND

BILL

A duck makes its feathers waterproof by rubbing them with a waxy oil from a gland near its tail called the preen gland. This oil repels water. Beneath the feathers is a lining of small fluffy feathers called down. The duck stays dry and warm.

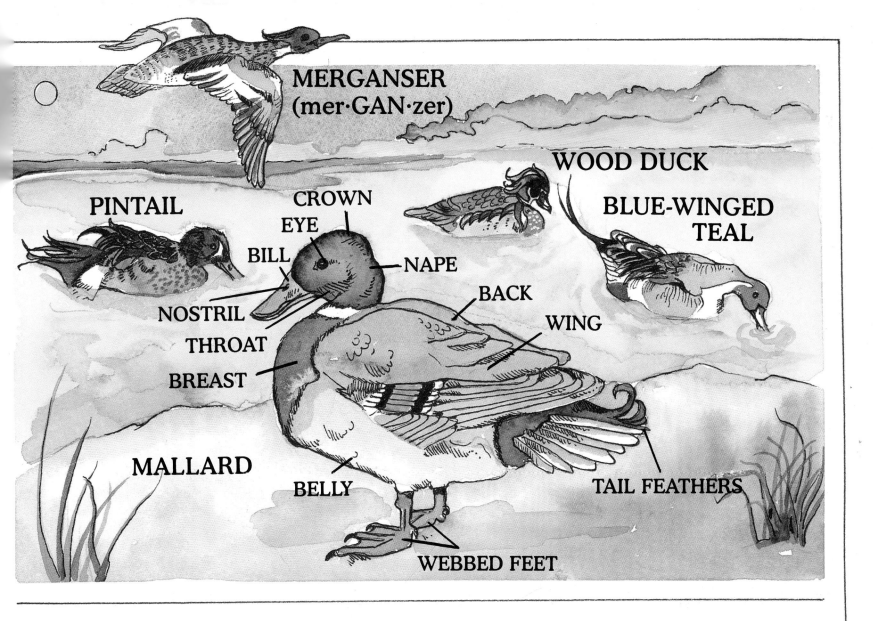

MERGANSER
(mer·GAN·zer)

WOOD DUCK

PINTAIL

BLUE-WINGED
TEAL

CROWN

EYE

BILL

NAPE

NOSTRIL

BACK

THROAT

WING

BREAST

MALLARD

BELLY

TAIL FEATHERS

WEBBED FEET

There are about 150 different kinds of ducks in the world. Some are small and others are big. Many are brightly colored and others are not, but they all have the same basic body shape and characteristics.

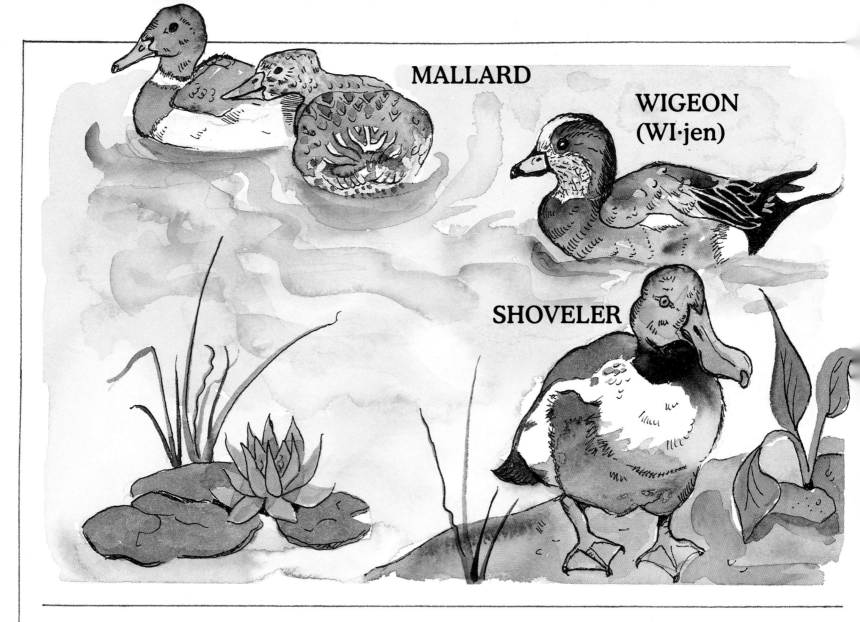

MALLARD

WIGEON
(WI·jen)

SHOVELER

Ducks live on every continent except Antarctica. About fifty different kinds of ducks live in North America. Many live near fresh water. They are found around ponds, swamps, streams, rivers, and lakes.

EIDER
(EYE·der)

MERGANSER

GOLDENEYE

OLDSQUAW

Others live near saltwater. Often they are called sea ducks and can be found out at sea as well as along ocean shores.

DABBLING DUCKS

WIGEON

BLACK
DUCK

Dabbling ducks use bony plates called LAMELLAE (la·MEL·ee) to strain food from the water. Their bills are short and broad.

Scientists have divided ducks into two groups based on what they eat. Both groups live near fresh water and saltwater. First there are dabbling ducks. They usually feed in shallow water with their heads underwater and their tails tipping up. Their food is close to the water's surface. They eat water plants, seeds, insects, and small creatures such as worms and snails.

PINTAIL

MALLARD

Dabbling ducks float high on the surface of the water. When taking off, they rise from the water quickly.

DIVING DUCKS

CANVASBACK

MERGANSER

MERGANSER DUCKS
have long narrow bills with
saw-toothed edges called
SERRATIONS (sare·A·shuns)
to catch and hold fish.

OLDSQUAW

The other group is diving ducks. They dive completely underwater for their food, often 10 to 25 feet (3 to 8 meters) below the surface. Their food includes water plants, fish, clams, and snails.

EIDER

HARLEQUIN
(HAR·la·kwin)

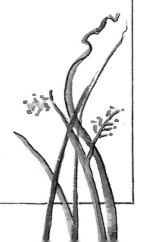

Diving ducks float lower in the water than dabbling ducks. Because they have small wings, before taking off they first must run along the surface of the water.

Ducks' legs are far back on their bodies. This makes them waddle when they walk on land, but it also makes them good at paddling and steering in the water.

Quack…quack… Ducks make sounds to communicate with each other. Most female ducks quack, squawk, or squeal. Males usually make softer whistling sounds, grunts, or coos.

Ducks MIGRATE when they go from one area to another with the change in seasons.

The ability to return to the same place year after year is called HOMING BEHAVIOR.

Sometimes ducks live in the same area year round. Others fly to warmer places for the winter. In the spring they return to the same place where they were hatched and raised.

Some ducks migrate short distances. Others fly thousands of miles, following the same route year after year. These routes are called flyways. The ducks stop at the same feeding grounds along the way.

DRAKES have colorful feathers.

HENS have less colorful feathers.

In the springtime most ducks return to their breeding grounds where they will mate and raise their young. The mallard is the most common duck in the world. Like other drakes, the mallard drake uses it colorful feathers to attract its mate. It also shows off by shaking its head and tail, and splashing water around with its bill.

NEST

Nest-building time begins. The mallard hen builds her nest on the ground using grasses, reeds, mosses, and leaves. Then she lines it with down feathers from her breast to make it soft. The drake protects the nesting territory from enemies.

A group of eggs is called a CLUTCH.

EGG

Soon the hen begins laying one egg a day, until there are ten to twelve eggs. She sits on the eggs to keep them warm so they can develop. This is called incubating. The color of her dull brown feathers blends in with her surroundings to keep her hidden from enemies. This is called camouflage. If she has to leave her nest, she covers her eggs with down to keep them warm and safe.

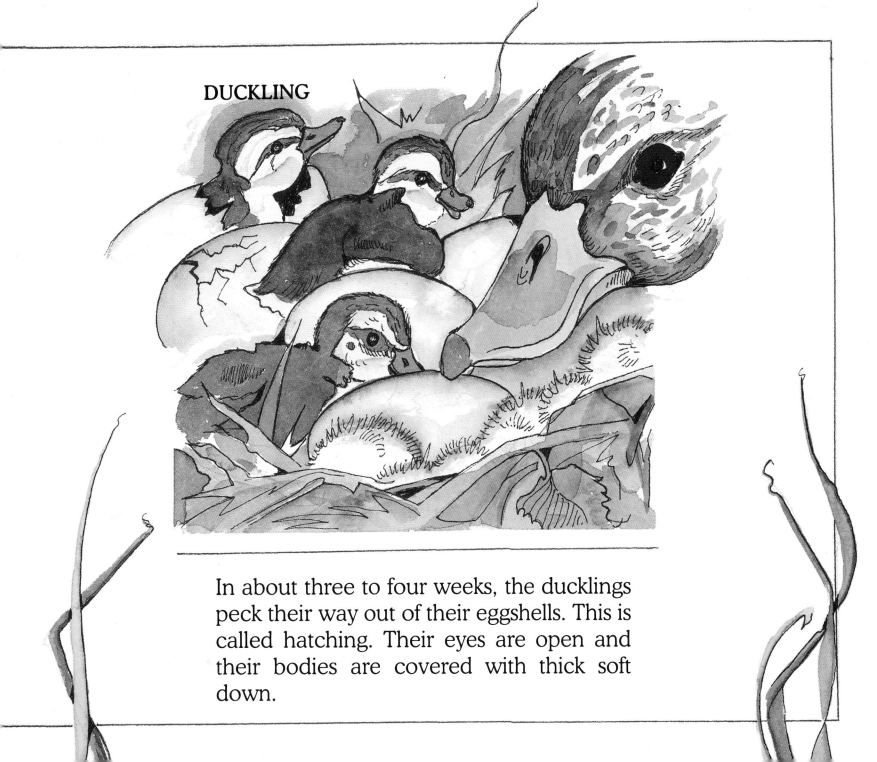

DUCKLING

In about three to four weeks, the ducklings peck their way out of their eggshells. This is called hatching. Their eyes are open and their bodies are covered with thick soft down.

Most of the time, the first moving thing a duckling sees is its mother. The duckling instinctively will follow her where she goes. When they are a few hours old, ducklings are ready to follow their mother, feed themselves, and begin swimming. The drake is gone. He doesn't help raise the young.

A group of ducklings is called a brood. The mother keeps her brood together and protects them from enemies such as raccoons, hawks, foxes, snapping turtles, and other animals.

The ducklings grow quickly. In about six weeks they have all their feathers. At about two months old, they are full grown and able to fly.

When winter begins to set in, they will be ready to fly south with the other ducks.

DOMESTICATED DUCKS

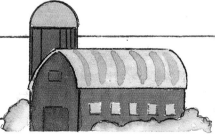

INDIAN
RUNNER

WHITE PEKIN
(PEE·kin)

KHAKI
(KAK·ee)
CAMPBELL

BUFF

ROUEN
(roo·AN)

About 1000 years ago people tamed and raised wild mallard ducks in China for their meat, eggs, and feathers. Today there are five kinds of ducks raised by farmers for food.

Some people raise ducks as pets. Sometimes they enter their ducks in contests or shows.

Throughout history, wild ducks have been hunted and their habitats have been destroyed. Many wetlands have been filled in to build homes, highways, and factories. Sometimes accidental oil spills coat their bodies and they die. In many areas there are fewer and fewer wild ducks.

Fortunately, many conservation groups are trying to protect wild ducks. Protected areas have been established along duck flyways and in other places.

Domesticated ducks can be seen and sometimes touched or fed at petting farms and zoos. Wild ducks can often be seen in parks.

It is fun to watch ducks and their fluffy little ducklings.

QUACK...QUACK...QUACK...

The first ducks lived about 80 million years ago.

In 1916 the United States and Canada signed the Migratory Bird Treaty to protect ducks.

Teal and bufflehead ducks are the smallest ducks. They are about 14 inches (35 cm) long and weigh about one pound (.45 kg). The biggest duck is the muscovy. It can be 35 inches (87 cm) long and can weigh 15 pounds (6.7 kg).

The blue-winged teal and the green-winged teal are the fastest ducks. They can fly up to 70 miles (112 km) an hour. The blue-winged teal flies from Canada to South America and back again when it migrates.

King eider ducks can dive as deep as 180 feet (55 m).

Some ducks, such as wood ducks, nest in holes in trees or in boxes made by people.

Scientists have learned about duck migration routes by putting small identification bands on their legs. This enables scientists and other people to report where the tagged ducks are in order to keep track of the population.

Ducks may live to be twenty years old.

A group of ducks is called a flock. When ducks swim together in a large group they are "rafting."

One very popular children's book is *Make Way for Ducklings* by Robert McCloskey.

NEVER try to feed or tame a wild duck! Its home is in nature.

If you ever are given a chance to hold a duckling at a petting zoo or farm, hold it gently. Speak to it quietly so it won't be scared.